D1472501

FAERIEGROUND IS PUBLISHED BY
STONE ARCH BOOKS
A CAPSTONE IMPRINT
1710 ROE CREST DRIVE
NORTH MANKATO, MINNESOTA 56003
WWW.CAPSTONEPUB.COM

COPYRIGHT © 2012 BY STONE ARCH BOOKS

ALL RIGHTS RESERVED. NO PART OF THIS
PUBLICATION MAY BE REPRODUCED IN
WHOLE OR IN PART, OR STORED IN A
RETRIEVAL SYSTEM, OR TRANSMITTED IN
ANY FORM OR BY ANY MEANS, ELECTRONIC,
MECHANICAL, PHOTOCOPYING, RECORDING,
OR OTHERWISE, WITHOUT WRITTEN
PERMISSION OF THE PUBLISHER.

LIBRARY OF CONGRESS CATALOGING-IN-
PUBLICATION DATA IS AVAILABLE ON THE
LIBRARY OF CONGRESS WEBSITE.

LIBRARY BINDING: 978-1-4342-3304-2

SUMMARY: SOLI AND LUCY LEARN MORE
ABOUT THE HISTORY OF FAERIEGROUND.

BOOK DESIGN BY K. FRASER
ALL PHOTOS © SHUTTERSTOCK WITH THESE
EXCEPTIONS: AUTHOR PORTRAIT © K FRASER
AND ILLUSTRATOR PORTRAIT © ODESSA
SAWYER

PRINTED IN THE UNITED STATES OF AMERICA
IN STEVENS POINT, WISCONSIN.
052013
007383R

> *"Wishes come true, not free."*
> – Stephen Sondheim, *Into the Woods*

For Valarie, who wished me away, and wished me home. -b
For the Fraser sisters: you are all a mother could wish for. -k

Long ago, a kingdom was founded in Willow Forest . . .

Now, hope has arrived. Two girls have entered the faerieground. One was wished there, and one followed.

One is the hope the faeries have waited for. The other is her best friend. One can fight for the kingdom, and one can help her.

But saving the faerie kingdom in Willow Forest won't be easy.

Chapter 1

Lucy

The willow queen shoots angry looks at me as the guard pushes me into her chambers.

I don't know what's going on.

Since Soli left with Kheelan, I've been locked
in my cell. I can't imagine why Queen
Calandra brought me back here to her rooms.

The queen slams the door in the guard's face.
Then she pushes me down onto the sofa.

Her eyes—Soli's eyes—are angry.

"You are Andria's daughter," she says. It isn't a
question.

"Yes," I say, sitting up straight. I am proud of my mother.

Queen Calandra's nostrils flare. "Your mother is a witch," she says. The way she spits out the word makes me afraid to laugh.

Instead, I picture my mother.

My mother, a witch?

My mother, the calm, sweet, loving woman I know. A nurse, a healer.

My mother—who has left offerings for the faeries as long as I can remember, sprigs of lavender, willowbuds, cattails, butterfly wings—a witch?

But I do know that she angered the queen, and I do know she'd never tell me why.

"She isn't a witch," I say, as bravely as I can. "She's a nurse."

Queen Calandra laughs. "Right," she says. "A nurse."

"She is!" I say. "She helps deliver babies and she takes care of sick kids."

The queen's face grows dark. Her eyes narrow. "I bet she takes care of kids," she says. "After all, she stole mine."

I can't help it. I glance up at the oil painting above the sofa.

The baby nestled in the queen's arms, like a blossom in its bud.

"Is—is that your baby?" I ask.

"Yes," the queen says. Then she laughs, an angry little laugh. "Or she was, anyway. Until your mother took her."

Then she tells me the story.

Chapter 2

Soli

Night is falling again.

Kheelan and I follow Motherbird through the forest toward Black Lake. I know this isn't my forest, really, but I can't shake the feeling that I know it. Like a place I visited in a dream.

"This way," Motherbird says, lifting a branch so that we can pass underneath it.

It's the first time she's spoken to me since we were in her tent. When she told me the Dark Crown belonged to me. I tried to get her to explain, but she wouldn't. I can't decide if she's crazy. Maybe everyone here is. Maybe I am.

Only I know I'm not.

As we walk, I finally have time to ask Kheelan
some of the things I've been wondering about.
Like: why didn't the queen just get the Dark
Crown for herself? Why do I have to go and
get it?

"She can't," he says. "They put a spell on it and
buried it deep." He glances at me and adds,
"And it's not hers, anyway."

I shudder. I haven't told him what Motherbird
said, that the crown is mine.

He'll think I'm crazy, or that she is. "Whose is it?" I ask, trying to act casual.

"You don't know any of our history?" he asks. Around us, the woods grow more open. I hear water, the rushing of a nearby river. We must be getting close.

"No," I say. "How would I? I mean, until yesterday——" I pause, trying to count the days since I wished Lucy away——"or the day before, I guess, I didn't even believe in faeries."

"Really?" Kheelan says, smiling. "Do you now?"

I laugh. "I think so," I say. Then I surprise myself. I reach out and touch his hand. His skin is warm, and it sends a delicious shiver through me.

He meets my eyes. "Real?" he asks in a low voice.

"Yes," I say.

Then we are quiet for a while.

Chapter 3

Lucy

Here is the story the willow queen tells me.

Once there was a kingdom. It was healthy and happy. The people who lived there were joyful. Things went wrong sometimes, but they solved their problems.

The queen of the kingdom had a baby, and the kingdom was full of joy. It was a beautiful baby girl. They named her Hope.

Then the king died. It was terribly sad. Unexpected. He had been a good king. He made the kingdom a good place to live. Everyone mourned him.

The queen didn't have time to cry. The kingdom needed a leader. She was the only one who could do it.

But some people in the kingdom, traitors, hated her. They wanted her power, or were jealous of it. They, with the help of the Ladybirds, outcasts who had left the kingdom generations ago, built up an army. And one night they came to the queen and they came into her rooms and they took the thing she loved the most. Her child. Her Hope. They stole the most valuable things the queen owned. The Dark Crown, and the royal seal.

They took the Dark Crown and buried it at the bottom of Black Lake. They tricked a human into diving down to hide it, because faeries can't swim. They knew the queen would never be able to retrieve the crown in its deep hiding spot.

And they took the baby and gave her to a witch, and they gave the witch a necklace. The royal seal was chained to it with faeriegold, which can't melt or burn or be broken by anyone but its owner. But the queen needed the royal seal and the Dark Crown. She needed them to restore the kingdom to power.

The queen, separated from her darling child, became so sad in her soul that she could barely move. The kingdom crumbled around her.

The rest of the people, saddened by the sight of the queen's unhappiness, became unhappy themselves. Everyone knew that all the queen needed was the Dark Crown and the royal seal. And her daughter. Then the kingdom would bloom again, would become the place it was meant to be, the place it had been before the king left it.

That is the story she tells me. And I know without being told that some of it must be a lie.

Chapter 4

Soli

I'm starting to think we'll never reach
the Black Lake.

Then, finally, we climb a small, grassy hill and pick our way through a stand of trees. Beyond it is water.

"The Black Lake," Motherbird says. "And your crown is beneath the water."

Kheelan looks at me. "Your crown?" he says, confusion darkening his face.

"That's right," Motherbird tells him. Then she looks at me and adds, "And you must be the one to retrieve it."

I look at the lake. It is black and churning.

I look back at Motherbird, but she is gone.

Kheelan shrugs. "The birds," he says. "They disappear."

I look at Black Lake again. "Am I supposed to just wear my clothes?" I ask.

"Do you have any choice?" Kheelan asks.

I open my backpack. Maybe there's a t-shirt in there, or a scarf, anything.

Just a jar of fireflies. I clasp the jar to my
chest, wishing. My wish is simple: *Help me.*

I open the jar and the lightning bugs swarm
out. I expect them to lead me somewhere, but
instead they move together. "They're weaving
something," Kheelan says. He doesn't seem
surprised.

After a moment, the fireflies disappear. The
jar is empty again. And at my feet lies a thick,
warm towel.

Without thinking, I dive deep into the water.

Chapter 5

Lucy

Back in my cell.

I've lost track of what time it is. I keep thinking about the queen's story. The dead king. The witch who is my mother. The stolen baby. Who is Soli, or is me. I need to know the real story.

And then, as if an answer, the door to my cell opens and a faerie girl is shoved inside. "I'll never tell!" she screams at the slamming door.

A key turns in a lock and we are alone. The girl turns to me. "Who are you?" she asks. She doesn't seem angry anymore, but her face is flushed.

"Um. I'm Lucy," I say.

She looks me up and down. "You're not from here," she says. "You're not one of us." Then she laughs.

"Why is that funny?" I ask.

The girl shrugs. "Because what does that mean, really," she says. "One of us. Who are we. You know?"

"The faeries?" I suggest.

"I suppose," she says. "But beyond that."

"What's your name?" I ask.

"Caro," she says. "Caro, the Betrayer."

"Who did you betray?" I ask.

"The kingdom, I suppose," she says. "The queen. You, if you're on her side."

"I don't even know what the sides are," I admit. "I don't trust the queen, but I don't know any other side of the story."

"You really aren't from around here, are you,"
Caro says, shaking her head. She unties the
cloth holding her hair up and it floats down
around her shoulders. It's light, like mine.

"No," I say, studying her. She's reminding me
of my mother. How strange.

"Will you tell me the other side of the story?"
I ask. I bite my lip. She's my only chance to
find out the truth.

Caro leans against the stone wall. Then she
tells me.

Chapter 6

Soli

The water is cold. The water is hot.

The water is hard. The water is soft.

I can't breathe. My arms and legs ache.

It's hard to get down to the bottom. It's hard to push through the water.

Beneath the water, far, far down, there is a metal box. And inside the metal box there is a wooden box. And inside the wooden box there is a velvet bag.

And inside the velvet bag there is a crown.

Chapter 7

Lucy

Here is the story Caro
tells me.

Once there was a kingdom built in a forest of willow trees. It was healthy and happy, though not perfect. Sometimes things went wrong. But problems were solved.

The king of the kingdom was lonely. Until he met a woman. Her name was Calandra. She was passing through the kingdom. No one knew where she was from or where she was going.

The willow king fell in love with her. They married. And right away, the kingdom changed.

Things began to go wrong. Problems couldn't be solved. The king seemed to disappear. The queen was cruel.

When the queen had a baby, there was hope in the kingdom. Perhaps the queen would learn to be kind. Perhaps the baby would bring life back to the kingdom.

Then the king died. He had never been sick, as far as anyone knew. There was no accident.

But that is a different story.

Once the king was gone, the queen was the only one in charge of the kingdom. Things went terribly wrong. She waged war on friends nearby. She took too much from everyone. People went hungry. People died. The people who tried to help her to see how things were falling apart—those people disappeared. Or they left. They joined a group of the oldest faeries, the Ladybirds, and they built an army.

And one night, they put their plan into action. They would save the kingdom by removing the princess.

So they came into Queen Calandra's rooms
and took the baby and brought her out of the
faerieground where she would be safe. They
gave her to a woman who could protect her.
And that woman found a family where the
baby could hide. Then the only thing keeping
the queen in power were the royal emblems.
The Dark Crown, and the royal seal. They
took the crown and sank it at the bottom
of Black Lake. And they gave the seal to the
woman protecting the baby. It would keep
the baby safer. It was her birthright. It did not
belong to the queen.

After that, the queen stayed in power. The Ladybirds and their army had done all they could. The faeries left in the kingdom needed to overthrow the queen, and to do that, they needed the princess. And the princess was just a baby. They needed to wait.

But the queen wanted the baby back. She knew that in order to stay in power, she needed to get her daughter on her side. Or the queen needed to kill her.

The kingdom crumbled around the willow queen, but she was still in control.

And once the princess returned, the queen would have all the power there was. She would retrieve the crown and the seal.

Everything would be in place.

So Queen Calandra waited. She waited for the daughter to get old enough to be angry.

This is the story Caro tells me. This time I believe each word.

Chapter 8

Soli

I am soaking wet when I climb out of the water.

Kheelan wraps my firefly towel around me.
He holds me close. The towel dries me quickly
and then dissolves.

"We should hurry," Kheelan says, looking up at
the sky. The light is fading. We only have until
tomorrow morning at sunrise.

"Thank you," I say. "For helping me," I say.
"For coming along."

He reaches out and smoothes my hair. "Of
course, princess," he says. Then he kisses me.
Then we run.

Chapter 9

Lucy

"The queen's story was different,"
I tell Caro.

"Of course it was," Caro says. She's dug a bit of chocolate out of her pocket, and we're sharing it. "That's how she works."

"I have a question," I admit. "Why did they put the crown under the lake? She told me it was because faeries couldn't swim. Is that true?"

Caro laughs, a short, angry laugh. "No," she says. "You have to have a little faerie blood to enter the Black Lake."

I stop eating. I look at her. "What?" I ask.

"The queen," she says. "She's not faerie. She's human. That's why she can't leave. Because she'd never be able to return. That's why they hid the crown. Because it was the only thing giving her power."

"Then why isn't she just overthrown?" I ask, confused.

Caro shrugs. "She's tricked everyone," she says. "She's a witch."

"She said my mother was a witch," I mutter.

Caro's head snaps up. "Your mother knows her?" she asks.

"I guess so," I say. "My mother told me a long time ago that she angered the queen. And the queen said that they gave the baby to my mother."

Caro stands, her face a picture of shock. "Then you're the baby," she says. "You're Hope. You're the princess."

- *Lucy* -

Chapter 10

Soli

Kheelon and I run

The whole time we run, a red hot rose blooms in my chest. The feeling of Kheelan's lips on mine.

Soon, the palace rises up in front of us. It is almost dawn.

Guards find us as soon as we enter the palace grounds. They snap us into chains and lead us to the throne room.

The queen sweeps in, eyes red. She looks tired. She looks angry.

She stares at me. "Where is it?" she asks. Not

asks. Demands. The chains disappear. The

queen crosses her arms. "Give me the crown,"

she says. "Now. Then you can see your friend."

I open my backpack. The velvet bag is inside.

"Wait," Kheelan whispers. "Make sure you get

what you want first."

I zip up my bag again. "Where is Lucy?" I ask.

"Give me the crown," the queen says.

I am afraid, but I try not to show it. "No," I say. The chains snap back onto my wrists.

"No?" the queen roars. "No?"

"No," I say again, my voice shaking. "Bring me my friend. Bring Lucy here."

Queen Calandra rolls her eyes. "Fine," she says. She points at one of the guards and says, "Bring me the girl."

The guard looks at me quickly, and I swear he winks. Then he's gone.

Queen Calandra taps her foot while we wait. "I suppose you saw the crazy loons," she says to Kheelan. "I'm sure they filled your heads with more nonsense."

Kheelan stands straight. "Not nonsense," he says. "But they filled our heads, yes. They led us to the lake. They told Soli what she was looking for and who it belongs to."

Then the queen's eyes narrow. She looks afraid. But she shakes it off. "So you dove down into Black Lake," she says to me. "Why aren't your clothes wet?"

I look down at myself. "I had a towel," I say.

The door to the throne room is thrown open.

A guard leads Lucy inside.

Chapter 11

Lucy

"Lucy!" Soli screams.

Though we're both in chains, we run to each other and try to hug. I'm so happy to see her. I'm so grateful that she found me.

But now I'm afraid. If I am the willow queen's daughter, like Caro thinks I am, what happens next? Do I have to stay here? Will she treat me better once she discovers who I really am?

The story makes sense. I was given to my mother for safekeeping. That explains why I've always felt like my mother didn't truly love me. That she cared more about Soli.

But I can't keep thinking about it. Soli is crying into my hair. "I'm here," I whisper. "Don't worry. I'll get you out of here."

Hands rip us apart. "Now give me the crown," Queen Calandra—my mother?—says, towering above us.

Soli glances at Kheelan. Then she takes my hand. "No," she says. "It belongs to me."

And she reaches into her backpack, pulls out a crown, and places it on her head.

Chapter 12

Soli

At first, the queen looks shocked.

Then she laughs. "You'll need more than just that dirty old crown," she says. "It's worthless on its own, daughter."

Daughter.

Lucy gasps. "Of course," she whispers. "Of course."

"Of course what?" I ask.

She laughs lightly. "Of course it isn't me," she says. "Never mind. I thought—never mind."

"Give it to me now," the queen says. "There's no point in you having it."

I take off the crown, turn it around in my hands. Now I can look at it in the light for the first time.

On one side, there's a small hole. As if something was there and then broken from it in a perfect circle. The size of the pendant Andria gave me.

Then I know what to do.

Chapter 13

Lucy

Soli reaches into her shirt and pulls out my mother's necklace.

She rips the chain from her throat, breaking it. Then she places the pendant into a hole on the side of the crown.

She places the crown on top of her own head.

Wings bud from her back.

Our chains melt.

Kheelan laughs. "Now you're you," he says. "Welcome home."

A guard whispers, "Princess."

Chapter 14

Soli

I look my mother in the eye, but she can't meet my gaze.

The guards kneel. Kheelan kneels.

"Who are you?" I ask.

Calandra looks down. "I'm the queen," she says, but now her voice is the one that shakes.

"Remove the glamour," Kheelan whispers. "Just wish it away."

"Don't," Calandra says. She's begging.

"I wish to remove the glamour on this woman," I say.

Her wings fall away. The queen moans. She's just a normal woman now, getting old, all alone.

Then I look at Lucy and say, "I wish to send my friend—"

"No!" Lucy yells.

"You have to go home, Lucy," I say. "Your mom is so worried."

"What about you?" Lucy asks. "What will you do?"

I look around. The castle is crumbling. The people who live here are afraid.

Kheelan stands and takes my hand. "There's work to be done here," he says.

"I have to stay," I tell Lucy.

"Then I will stay too," says Lucy. "I'll help you." Tears fall from her eyes.

"We should ask your mom," I say, like I've said a million times before—about dinners, playtimes, movies, sleepovers.

Lucy and I laugh. She takes my hand. "We'll ask my mom," she says. "And then I'll help you."

We have always been together, Lucy and I. She was the brave one. I was the fearful one.

Not anymore.

Together, we step back through the willow queen's gate.

Bracken, Beth.
The Willow Queen's gate

RECEIVED JAN - - 2014